MARC BROWN

Arthur's Lost Duckling

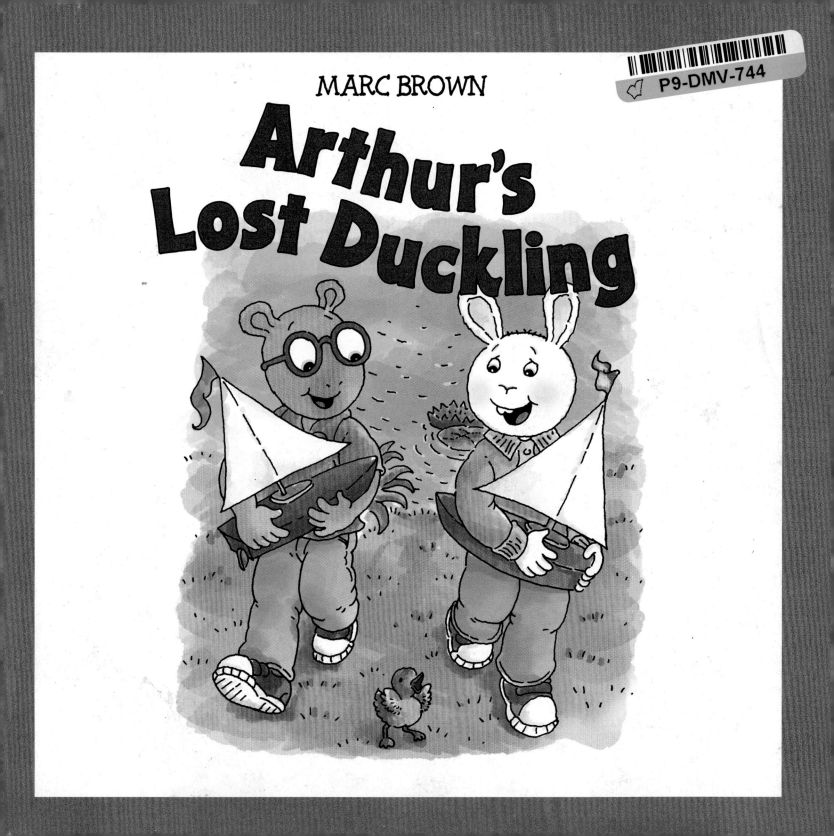

Arthur and Buster were sailing boats.

"Look at the ducks," said Arthur.

"I bet they could use a snack," said Buster.

They tossed some crackers into the water.

The littlest duck swam over to Arthur and Buster.

Arthur tossed him some crackers.

"He's so cute!" said Buster.

When the crackers were gone, the ducks swam away.

Later Arthur and Buster noticed the box of crackers began quacking.

"It's one of the ducklings," said Buster.

"He's all alone," said Arthur. "Let's take him home."

Arthur took the duckling home on his bike.

"He thinks he's flying," said Buster.

"Bye, little guy," said Buster. "See you in the morning."

"See you, Buster," said Arthur.

"I'm home!" said Arthur. "And I have a surprise."

"Quack!" said the duckling.

"Can I keep him?" asked Arthur. "His mother left him in the park."

"He's so cute!" D.W. said.

"He needs to be free," Mom explained. "But I guess he can stay here tonight."

"It's okay, Pal," said Arthur. "He won't bite."

Pal sniffed the duckling.

"Quack," said the duckling.

Soon the duckling followed Pal everywhere.

Arthur filled the tub with water. The duckling splashed
and shook his feathers.

"I'm not taking my bath with a duck!" said D.W.

Later, Arthur made a little nest for the duckling.

"Tomorrow, I'll teach you to fly," said Arthur. "Then Mom will see how happy you are here, and she'll let me keep you."

"Dream on," said D.W.

Buster came over the next morning.

"Time for a flying lesson!" said Arthur.

He and Buster ran around, jumping and flapping their arms.

The duckling just watched.

"He needs a good breakfast," said Buster.

But the duckling didn't eat.

"I think he's sad!" D.W. said.

"We need some advice from the Brain," said Arthur.

The Brain arrived with his remote control blimp.

"He's going to love this!" said the Brain.

The blimp soared through the air.

"Don't you want to fly like that?" said Arthur.

But the duckling just looked at him.

"I think he's homesick," said D.W.

"Let's look for his family at the lake,"
 said Arthur.

"How can he follow his family?" said Buster.
"He can't fly."

"I have an idea," said Arthur.

They worked on Arthur's idea all day.

Then Arthur's dad drove them to the lake.

"What is it?" D.W. asked.

"It's a glider," said Arthur.

"It looks like a duck," said D.W.

Arthur threw the glider into the air.

"Come on," he said. "Fly!"

The duckling flapped his wings, but nothing happened.

"It's not working," said D.W.

"You can do it," said Arthur.

The duck flapped his wings, and
this time he took off.

The glider fell to the ground.
But the duckling continued to fly.

They all heard a quack.
Then many quacks. It was the
mother duck and her ducklings.

"Look!" said D.W. "She knows it's her baby."

"We did it!" said Arthur. "He's back with his family."

"Hooray!" said D.W. "Now I can take a bath."